Just the Way You Are

igloobooks

This igloo book belongs to:

....

igloobooks

Published in 2020
by Igloo Books Ltd
Cottage Farm
Sywell
NN6 0BJ
www.igloobooks.com

Illustrated by Daniel Howarth
Written by Alex Michaels

Cover designed by Lee Italiano
Interiors designed by Jason Shortland
Edited by Natalia Boileau

0220 004
6 8 10 12 11 9 7 5
ISBN 978-1-78440-726-1

Printed and manufactured in China

Even though we're different, I think that you're a **star**.
In fact, you're simply **perfect**, just the way you are.

Mouse

I am fast and you are slow but we have **fun** together.

We **always** go outside and play,
no matter what the weather.

I know that **friends** like us make a very unlikely pair.

I just **want** you to know
that I really, truly care.

I was wondering why I **like** you and now I can see why.
It's because you make me so happy, I feel like I can **fly**.

Even though you're **spiky**, you've got a **heart** of gold.

I **hope** that we'll be friends
until we're **really** old.

Sometimes you're very **cheeky,**
but I **love** you all the same.

The **best** time of the day is when we play our **special** game.

I'm not sure **why** I like you.
It must be all your **charm**.

Sometimes you can be **scary**, but I know I'm **safe** from harm.

Even though we like different things, I **love** you anyway.

You're the **only** one I want
to play with every day.

I just want to say to you that I'm **proud** you are my friend.

We may not be the **same,** but we'll make it in the end.

Others might think it's **funny** when they see us together.
We just **smile** because we know we'll be friends forever.